# Beautiful Little Black Girl

Written by Ruth Obryant
Illustrated by Aubrey Scott

For Niya, Kayla, Faith, Jamiah and Lillie, my five beautiful little black girls.
-R.O.

Imagination & Me Press
Copyright © 2022 by Ruth O'Bryant
All rights reserved, including the right to reproduction in whole or in part in any form without written permission except in the case of brief quotations embodied in critical articles or reviews.

Imagination & Me Press, LLC
1215 N. Military HWY
# Box 241
Norfolk, VA 23502

Publisher's Cataloging-in-Publication data
Names: O'Bryant, Ruth, author. | Scott, Aubrey, illustrator.
Title: Beautiful little Black girl / Ruth O'Bryant; illustrated by Aubrey Scott.
Description: Norfolk, VA: Imagination & Me Press LLC, 2022.| Summary: When six-year-old Maya questions the beauty of her dark skin, her family lovingly affirms the brilliance, beauty, diversity, and legacy of her beautiful melanin skin.
Identifiers: LCCN: 2022900018 | ISBN: 978-1-7374723-1-5 (hardcover) | 978-1-7374723-0-8 (paperback)
Subjects: LCSH African American girls--Juvenile fiction. | African Americans--Juvenile fiction. | Girls--Juvenile fiction. | Families--Juvenile fiction. | Self-esteem--Juvenile fiction. | Conduct of life--Juvenile fiction. | BISAC JUVENILE FICTION / People & Places / United States / African American & Black
Classification: LCC PZ7.1 .O197 Be 2022 | DDC [E]--dc23

**Beautiful, Little Black Girl, what do you see when you look in the mirror?**

In you, I see grace. I see true beauty, from the coils in your hair to the bend of your toes.

Beautiful, Little Black Girl, what do you see when you look in the mirror?

In you, I see God's majesty, love, goodness, and strength.

**Beautiful, Little Black Girl, what do you see when you look in the mirror?**

In you, I see our history, legacy, and future.

**Beautiful, Little Black Girl, your skin sparkles and shines ebony, mahogany, caramel,**

**toffee, chocolate swirl, brown sugar, ruddy red, and honey...**

Phenomenal, Little Black Girl, your hair . . . your beautiful coiled hair!

**Wear it however you dare, up, down, braids, ponytails, afro puffs, or wild!**

Extraordinary, Little Black Girl, your eyes shine as if they hold the sun, moon, and stars. Oh, how beautiful they are!

**Magnificent, Little Black Girl, there is power in the fullness of your lips, arch of your eye-brows, strength of your**

cheek-bones, and the shape of your nose. Go ahead, strike a pose!

**My sweet Princess, you are more valuable than silver and gold.**

**You are more precious than diamonds and rubies. When God created you, He made you priceless.**

**Resilient, Little Black Girl, there is rhythm in your steps and a delightful melody in the sound of your voice!**

**Respectful, Little Black Girl, honor your**

mother and father.

Young lady, be polite and kind. Respect your elders. Use words such as yes, no, please, excuse me, and thank you.

**Brilliant, Little Black Girl, strive for excellence.**

Fall in love with math, reading, writing, science, and the Arts! Dream big! Reach for the stars!

Beautiful, Little Black Girl,
I Love You!



Amazing, Little Black Girl,
I Am So Proud Of You!

Amazing, Little Black Girl, wisdom is precious. Truth is powerful.

*Forgiveness is healing*

*Dreams are obtainable*

*Love is patient & kind*

**Forgiveness is healing. Dreams are obtainable. Love is patient and kind. God is love.**

**Marvelously wonderful,**

**Little Black Girl, what do you see when you look in the mirror?**

**I see God's perfect design!**

Made in the USA
Middletown, DE
20 January 2024

48184247R00024